For Trefor and Ceri

Library of Congress Cataloging in Publication Data

Watts, Bernadette.
　Rapunzel.

　　Summary:　Retells the tale of the beautiful
girl imprisoned in a lonely tower by a witch.
　　[1.　Fairy tales.　2.　Folklore—Germany]　I.
Grimm, Jakob Ludwig Karl, 1785-1863. Rapunzel.
II.　Title.
PZ8.W34Rap　　[398.2] [E]　　　75-8847
ISBN 0-690-00979-8
ISBN 0-690-00980-1 (lib. bdg.)

1　　2　　3　　4　　5　　6　　7　　8　　9　　10

Printed in Switzerland

Rapunzel

By the Brothers Grimm

Retold and Illustrated by
Bernadette Watts

Thomas Y. Crowell Company
New York

Once upon a time there lived a man and his wife who loved each other very much. The wife was expecting a child, and they looked forward with great happiness to its birth, for they had wanted a child for a long time. These good people had a little window at the back of their house, which looked into the loveliest garden, full of all kinds of beautiful flowers and vegetables; but the garden was not theirs. It was surrounded by a high wall, and no one dared to go into it, for it was owned by a witch who was feared by everyone in the whole world.

One day the wife stood looking out of her kitchen window. She could see over the wall and into the witch's garden, and growing there she saw some rapunzel lettuce. The leaves of this lettuce looked so tender and fresh and green that she longed to eat them. This desire grew stronger every day, but of course she knew that she could not have any because it belonged to the witch. Soon she became quite pale and ill from thinking about it. Finally her husband grew worried and asked,

"What is the matter, dear wife?"

"Oh," she answered, "if I don't get some rapunzel lettuce to eat out of the garden behind the house, I know I am going to die."

The man, who loved her dearly, thought to himself, Come, now, you cannot let your sweet wife die! You *must* get her some of this special lettuce, no matter what the cost. So that evening, when it was growing dark, he climbed over the wall into the witch's garden and, hastily gathering a handful of the lettuce leaves, he returned with them to his wife. She made them into a salad, which tasted so good that her longing for the forbidden food, instead of being satisfied, was greater than ever. So there was nothing for it but that her husband should climb over the wall again and bring her some more. So the next evening over he went, but this time when he reached the other side he shrank back in terror. For there, standing before him, was the old witch herself. She glared at him.

"How dare you climb into my garden and steal my rapunzel lettuce like a thief?" she demanded. "You shall be punished for this."

"Oh, please forgive me," he begged. "I had to do it. My dear wife saw your delicious-looking lettuce from her window, and she had such a desire for it that she certainly would have died if her wish had not been granted." On hearing this, the witch was a little less angry, and she said,

"Very well, if your wife's life depends on it, then you may take as much of my lettuce as you like, but on one condition only—that you give me the child your wife will soon bring into the world. You need not worry about it; I will look after it like a mother."

The man was so afraid of the witch that he agreed to everything she asked. And when their child was born and the witch appeared to claim it, he and his wife had no choice but to give the baby to her.

The witch named the child Rapunzel, after her lettuce.

Rapunzel was the most beautiful child under the sun, and at first the witch took very good care of her, as she had promised.

But on Rapunzel's twelfth birthday the witch shut her up in a tower in the middle of a deep forest. The tower had neither stairs nor doors. Even the windows were all sealed shut except for one, high up near the top.

When the old witch wanted to get in she would stand below the window and call out,

"Rapunzel, Rapunzel,

Let down your hair,"

for Rapunzel had wonderful long hair, as fine as spun gold. Whenever she heard the witch's voice, she made her hair into long braids like two ropes, and let them hang down out of the window. The old witch took hold of the ends, and Rapunzel pulled her up.

After they had lived like this for a few years, it happened one day that a prince was riding through the forest and passed by the tower. As he came near, he heard someone singing so sweetly that he stood still and listened, spellbound. It was Rapunzel in her loneliness trying to while away the time by letting her sweet voice ring out into the forest. The prince longed to see the owner of the voice but he could not find any door in the tower. He rode home, but his heart was so moved by the song he had heard that he returned every day to the forest and listened.

One day, when he was
standing there behind a tree, he
saw the old witch approach and
heard her call out,
    "Rapunzel, Rapunzel,
Let down your hair."
    Then Rapunzel let down her
braids and pulled the witch up.

"So that's the staircase to the tower!" said the prince. "Then I too will climb it."

So the next day, when it was growing a little dark, he went to the foot of the tower and called,

"Rapunzel, Rapunzel,
Let down your hair,"
and as soon as she had let it down the prince seized it and climbed up lightly.

At first Rapunzel was terribly frightened when the prince came in, for she had never seen a man before. But the prince spoke to her very kindly and told her at once that his heart had been so moved by her singing that he had wanted to see her. He was so gentle that Rapunzel soon forgot her fears, and when he asked her to marry him she agreed. For, she thought, he is young and handsome, and I'll certainly be happier with him than with the old witch. So she put her hand in his and said,

"Yes, I will gladly go with you."

But still there was the problem of how she would get down from the tower.

"I have an idea," said Rapunzel. "Every time you come to see me you must bring a skein of silk with you. I will weave them together into a ladder, and when it is finished I will climb down by it, and you will take me away on your horse."

They arranged that, until the ladder was ready, the prince would come to see her every evening. He did this, and soon he and Rapunzel were deeply in love. The old witch, of course, knew nothing of what was going on, because she came to see Rapunzel only during the daytime.

However, one day Rapunzel, not thinking of what might happen, turned to the witch and said,

"How is it, Godmother, that you seem so much heavier to pull up than the young prince? He is always with me in a moment."

"Oh, you wicked child," cried the witch. "What is this I hear? I thought I had hidden you safely from the whole world, and still you have managed to deceive me!"

Furious, the witch seized Rapunzel's beautiful hair and, winding it around and around her left hand, she picked up a pair of scissors in her right. Snip! Snap! the sharp blades of the scissors cut, and the long, lovely, golden hair lay on the floor. The witch was pitiless in her anger. She took Rapunzel far away to a deserted part of the forest and there she left her to live in loneliness and misery.

That evening, after she had driven poor Rapunzel away, the witch fastened the golden braids of hair to a hook in the window. When the prince came and called out, as usual,

"Rapunzel, Rapunzel,

Let down your hair,"

she let down the braids. The prince climbed up, but instead of his beloved Rapunzel he found the old witch, who fixed her evil, glittering eyes upon him and cried mockingly,

"Ah-hah! You thought you would find your ladylove, but the pretty bird has flown and it sings no more. The cat has caught it, and will scratch out your eyes, too. Rapunzel is lost to you forever. You will never see her again."

The prince was beside himself with grief, and, despairing, he jumped right out of the window, meaning to kill himself. He was not killed, however, as he fell into a bush, but his eyes were pierced by two thorns, so that he could not see.

Blind and miserable, he wandered for a whole year through the forest, weeping in sorrow for his lost bride.

At last, by chance, he came to the part of the forest where
Rapunzel was living.

Suddenly he heard a sweet voice singing a sad song. The voice was strangely familiar to him. As quickly as he could, he made his way toward the sound. As soon as Rapunzel saw him, she ran to him and kissed him, weeping for joy. Two of her tears fell on his eyes, and instantly they were healed, and he could see as clearly as he ever had.

Then the prince led Rapunzel to his kingdom, where they were welcomed with great joy. In due time they had twin children, a boy and a girl, and they all lived happily for many years to come.

Bernadette Watts, though born in England, has spent much time in Germany, Switzerland, and other countries of Europe, and has a special fondness for the classic European folktales. Her illustrations for this book are executed in a combination of pastel and tempera. Though lushly impressionistic and imaginative, they are firmly based on the actual architecture, scenery, and traditional peasant costume of the area from which this version of the story of Rapunzel comes. Ms. Watts has illustrated three other tales by the brothers Grimm as well as some other classics and has also written and illustrated several books of her own. She grew up in the lovely English countryside not far from London, and now lives in Cornwall.

Variations of the story of Rapunzel appear in many European languages, and the story was, of course, already old when the brothers Grimm first set it down for children in their *Hausmärchen* in 1812. Its theme of the poor but beautiful maiden imprisoned by an evil witch or sorcerer and rescued, after some difficulty, by a prince who loves her truly is a classic and recurrent one, of which there are many versions.

Jakob (1785-1863) and Wilhelm (1786-1859) Grimm were both distinguished philologists. But their fame rests less on their scholarly works than on their wonderful collections of folk literature. The *Hausmärchen* were published in Germany during the period 1812-1824. From that time on, these stories of familiar and lovable animals and people, of sparse peasant life or princely splendor, of brave deeds and strange adventures have brought delight to children all over the world.